E
Col
Colorado, Nani
Harry's mealtime mess

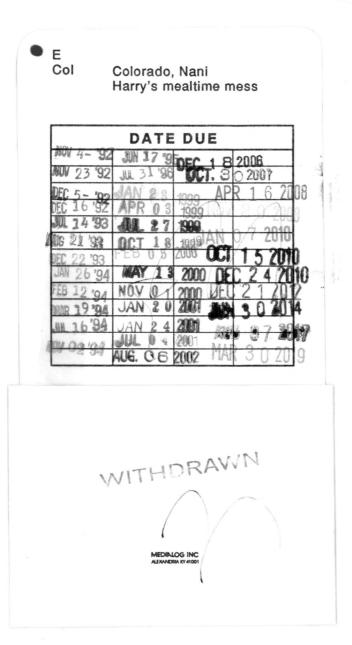

DATE DUE		
NOV 4 - '92	JUN 17 '95	DEC 1 8 2006
NOV 23 '92	JUL 31 '98	OCT. 3 0 2007
DEC 5 - '92	JAN 2 8 1999	APR 1 6 2008
DEC 16 '92	APR 0 3 1999	NOV 2 0 2008
JUL 14 '93	JUL 2 7 1999	JAN 0 7 2010
AUG 21 '93	OCT 1 8 1999	
DEC 22 '93	FEB 0 3 2000	OCT 1 5 2010
JAN 26 '94	MAY 1 3 2000	DEC 2 4 2010
FEB 12 '94	NOV 0 1 2000	DEC 2 1 2012
MAR 19 '94	JAN 2 0 2001	JUN 3 0 2014
JUL 16 '94	JAN 2 4 2001	APR 0 7 2017
NOV 02 '94	JUL 0 4 2001	MAR 3 0 2019
	AUG. 0 6 2002	

HARRY THE HIPPO

HARRY'S Mealtime Mess

Story by Nani Colorado
Illustrations by Jesús Gabán

Gareth Stevens Children's Books
MILWAUKEE

"It's mealtime, Harry,"
calls Mama. But Harry
just wants to play.

2

"I'm not hungry, Mama."

"But Harry, I made your
favorite lunch. Macaroni
and cheese . . .

. . . and orange juice!"
"Yuck! I don't like
macaroni and cheese!"

Harry would rather play
with his food than eat it.

6

"I'll just make a little train
with the noodles . . .

7

. . . and I'll put some in
my orange juice."

"Uh-oh! Now look at
the mess I've made!"

9

"I'd better clean it up before Mama comes!"

"Harry, what a big
mess you've made
in so little time!"

11

"Oh, no! A butterfly has
come to steal my lunch!"

"This macaroni and
cheese is mine!" SPLAT!

13

"Mama, the butterfly was
trying to eat my lunch . . .

14

. . . and you know that
macaroni and cheese
is my favorite meal!"

For a free color catalog describing Gareth Stevens' list of high-quality children's books, call 1-800-341-3569 (USA) or 1-800-461-9120 (Canada).

Library of Congress Cataloging-in-Publication Data

Gabán, Jesús.
    [Papouf n'a pas faim. English]
    Harry's mealtime mess / written by Nani Colorado ; illustrated by
Jesús Gabán. -- North American ed.
        p. cm. -- [Harry the hippo]
    Translation of : Papouf n'a pas faim. / Jesús Gabán, Nani Colorado.
    Summary: Harry the hippo would rather play with his macaroni than
eat it, but then he makes quite a mess defending it from a butterfly.
    ISBN 0-8368-0717-0
    [1. Hippopotamus--Fiction. 2. Food habits--Fiction. 3. Pasta products
--Fiction.] I. Colorado, Nani. II. Title. III. Series: Gabán, Jesús. Harry the hippo.
    PZ7.G1116Has   1991
    [E]—dc20   91-12869

North American edition first published in 1992 by

Gareth Stevens Children's Books
1555 North RiverCenter Drive, Suite 201
Milwaukee, Wisconsin 53212, USA

U.S. edition copyright © 1992. Text copyright © 1992 by Gareth Stevens, Inc.
First published in France, copyright © 1991 by Gautier-Languereau.

English text by Eileen Foran
Cover design by Beth Karpfinger and Sharone Burris

Printed in the United States of America

1 2 3 4 5 6 7 8 9 9 97 96 95 94 93 92